I'LL NEVER FORGET WHATSHISNAME AGAIN

Larry Geoghegan

Published by New Generation Publishing in 2018

First Edition

www.newgeneration-publishing.com

Contents

I'll Never Forget Whatshisname Again

I can't remember how long I've had a bad memory, perhaps I was born with this defect, although I'm not completely devoid of the ability to remember such things as birthdays, phone numbers, and appointments; in this respect my memory is average. No, the fault lies in not being able to remember faces, or to be more specific, being able to put a name to a face that I recognise. Sometimes this can be embarrassing.

I was leaving the bank where I work when a man calls out 'Hi Larry how are you?' There in front of me was a person whose face was familiar to me, but I could neither recall his name nor where I had met him. We carried on chatting, with him doing most of the talking and me making noises of agreement hoping that there would be some clue in his conversation which would strike a memory chord. Then he touched on the weather, saying he'd hope the rain would ease off because he wanted to mow the lawns. I said, 'Oh do you have a big garden? There was a surprised look on his face then he started to smile, 'I don't believe it, I get the distinct impression you don't know who I am. Am I right?' I felt quite embarrassed as I told him that I couldn't remember where I had seen him before. To which he answered, 'I'm Colin, your next-door neighbour, just wait until I tell Pauline.'

When I got home Pauline, my wife, saw the funny side and told me, 'At least you don't have to worry if you'll get Alzheimer's disease, because nobody will notice any difference.' After that I made a point of acknowledging anyone who said hello, waved or even nodded to me. Unfortunately this type of behaviour has its drawbacks. I was waiting for a train at Formby station. I had just missed one, so the platform was fairly empty when a woman on the platform opposite suddenly starts to shout and wave to me, so I waved back saying something like it was nice to see you again, but she interrupted me, 'Oh I'm sorry I wasn't waving at you, it's my daughter who is standing just behind you.'

Would I have to suffer the embarrassment of my forgetfulness for the rest of my life'? But help was at hand. Pauline bought me a book entitled *How to Improve Your Memory* by a leading memory expert (I've forgotten his name). The book contained methods of remembering playing card sequences, phone numbers, shopping lists and above all, as far as I was concerned, putting names to faces. Hurriedly I turned to the chapter on 'How to recall names and faces'. The system proved to be quite simple. When you first meet someone link his or her name to a facial feature. For example if Mr Bridges has hair growing from one eyebrow to the next then make an image of a large bridge. If Mrs Lomax has a protruding bottom lip visualise it hanging very low with, a raincoat attached to it. If the name is Evans try to see the person with a large halo over their head. It doesn't matter that the words Heaven and Evans are not the same, so long as it helps your memory.

I was looking forward to work the following day when I would be able to try out this system and in time I would be addressing every person by their name, much to the surprise and admiration of the rest of the staff. The following morning I started to give the customers' faces extra scrutiny and, as the morning progressed, I had to open an account for a new customer. Her name was Mrs Cole and she had wide nostrils so I imagined fire coming out of her nose. Fire, despite the difference in spelling, would give 'Cole'. After a while I became tired of my new found activity. I was losing interest in it. Besides the concentration in trying to imagine what objects fitted a person's features was affecting my work, so I gave it up.

About three weeks passed and this Mrs Cole came into the bank. I was pleased to say that I saw fire coming out of her hooter and felt she would be more than surprised when I addressed her by her name. She wasn't surprised; in fact she was a bit puzzled, when I said to her 'Good morning Mrs Burns.

You know I really must sit down and read that book again, if only I could remember where I put it!

Tomorrow's News

'Hi Charlie what's the news today?'

Old Charlie the paper seller smiled at Frank. 'It's fresh off the press today, young man.'

Frank paid for his paper, thanked the old man and hurried into the pub for his lunch. Inside he met his friend Tony.

'Hey Tony, you look a bit sorry for yourself. What's wrong?'

Tony pulled a face and said, 'To put it bluntly I've been booted out! It's this credit crunch. They need to reduce staff to improve profitability. It makes you sick.'

'Yes I know how you feel. I'll ask if there are any vacancies at our place, but with this recession no one feels safe.'

Frank ordered a meal and started to read his paper. Wait a minute, did you know there's a job going at this pub? "Wanted urgently barperson/waiter Union rates and gratuities".'

'Well no time like the present, I'll apply now.' Tony went to the bar and after a short conversation with the barman he came back looking puzzled.

'He didn't think there were any vacancies.'

As he sat down a loud crash could be heard all over the pub followed by an angry voice shouting, 'That's the second time this week, you clumsy sod. Put your coat on and get out. You're fired.'

The chef came out and spoke to the barman saying, 'When you have a moment Fred would you ring up the local paper and put in an advert for a new barman.'

Frank grabbed his newspaper and looked at the date. 'Good God it's got tomorrow's date.'

Tony studied the paper very carefully and said, 'You know, Frank, this isn't a misprint it appears genuine. Where did you get it?'

'Never mind that,' said Frank, 'Drink up we're going to the bookies.'

'You're not suggesting that it has today's winners in it are you?'

'I'm not suggesting anything but it's worth a small bet just to see what happens.'

The two of them entered the bookmakers giggling with anticipation like a pair of excited schoolboys. They decided to put £5 on a horse running at Haydock which the newspaper showed as a winner. It won. The next race they again backed a horse the paper showed as a winner. That too was first past the post. The third race proved the paper was right again. By this time the other occupants were crowding round the boys anxious to find out the name of their next selection. When the fourth winner romped home, the cheer from the punters was like a football crowd seeing their team score.

The staff were getting quite concerned and Frank, who was beginning to feel nervous, whispered to Tony, 'Let's go to another betting shop, the manager is getting suspicious.' Tony agreed and as they left the premises they were followed by a small army of gamblers all wanting to know what horse the two lads were going to pick.

When they arrived at the next bookmakers they were evidently expected. Two well-built men barred their entrance. The mob behind the boys began to grow ugly which prompted the manager to threaten them if they did not disperse he would ring the police. Frank and Tony decided to call it a day. 'After all,' said Frank, 'we have won over a grand,' but Tony wasn't satisfied.

'Christ, Frank, this is our big chance. Instead of going to the bookies next time we'll go to the race course and put our bets on with the Tote.'

'What do you mean next time? Do you think there's an unlimited supply of tomorrow's news?' Tony then agreed that he was taking things for granted.

Frank wended his way home and he went over the day's developments. Tony and Frank had won a £1000 between them and he thought he would invite Ann, his girlfriend out for a really good meal to celebrate, but where? He spread the newspaper out on the table and looked for the leisure guide and noticed a small piece of news:

MAN STABBED TO DEATH

> Frank Williams, 19, was attacked by burglars last night in his home. It is believed the victim was in possession of a sum of money, being the proceeds of winning bets at the local bookmakers. The thugs broke into his house shortly after six o'clock yesterday evening.

While he was reading the news item, Frank heard the sound of breaking glass and the forced opening of a window...

Stop Press News

Vernon Hamilton was the type of man who had few enemies and even less friends. He was a bank manager in a medium suburban branch and had just been informed that he was to be promoted to manager of a large city branch. Not only did this mean a big increase in his salary but also greater fringe benefits, such as a more expensive car, automatic membership of a much sought after golf club in the area and a liberal expense account.

At 40 years of age he was comparatively young to gain such a promotion and since he was not due to take up his new appointment until the end of the month he was journeying to the West Country for a fortnight's holiday.

Vernon took a sideways look at his reflection in the train window. 'Yes just a hint of a double chin and my hair is going grey at the temples, but that makes a man distinguished doesn't it? Christ I wish I could get rid of my paunch. Pity Ann was no longer alive she would have been overjoyed with my promotion, but she also had her feet on the ground. If I was getting 'too big for my boots' as she put it, a few chosen home truths would bring me back to earth. Then on the other hand if I felt low she could bolster my confidence.'

His thoughts were not only about his late wife, but also about when he first started work in the bank as a raw teenager. He'd passed the Institute of Bankers examinations in only three years. His companions took much longer; some even gave them up as being beyond their capabilities. One asset which helped in Vernon's career, was his unwavering honesty. He never tried to cover up his mistakes, not because he was highly moral or religious but because it was silly to risk his job for a temporary gain.

He recalled once seeing a middle-aged housewife being apprehended by security for shoplifting in a supermarket. The woman had entered the store without a basket or trolley, drawing attention to herself. If she meant to steal, wouldn't it have been more sensible to pretend to be a normal shopper? He never found out how much she was fined by the court but whatever it was it wasn't enough; she should have been fined for stupidity!

During his time in the bank he had come across a few attempts by members of the staff to defraud, always with the same belief that they could beat the system but to their cost they found they could not.

The train pulled into the station and the seaside resort outside was full of joy and sunshine. Vernon decided to forego the luxury of a taxi and walk the short distance to his hotel. When he unpacked he discovered he'd forgotten his shaving kit. No bother, there must be a shop nearby where he could purchase such items.

Vernon entered the supermarket pulling a basket from the pile and walked up and down the aisles looking for men's toiletries. Shaving soap, razors and aftershave lotion soon nestled at the bottom of his basket, when he decided to favour himself with a nightcap before turning in that night. He headed for the vast array of alcohol beverages and soon found his favourite tipple, brandy, in various sized bottles. Some large, half size and quarter size. Just handy to slip in your inside jacket pocket. 'Good God, what am I thinking of?' Despite the fact that he still had an untouched bottle of brandy in his hotel room he placed the small bottle into the basket.

He moved away from the drinks shelves but the thought of pocketing the brandy would not leave him. 'It would only be as an experiment. I could come back later, apologise and pay for the bottle.' He turned into the next aisle which was unusually crowded as he was jostled against the shelves of produce, he found himself quickly palming the brandy and slipping it into his inside pocket.

Vernon extricated himself from the swirling mass of customers and moved towards a line of busy checkout cashiers. His heart was pumping fast with a mixture of fear and excitement. Something inside of him told him to take the bottle out of his pocket and put it with his other purchases, but he disregarded his own advice, the thrill of beating the system was too strong. As nonchalantly as he could, he emptied the contents of his basket onto the conveyor belt, put the empty basket in the place provided and with a smile watched the young girl tallying up his goods.

He walked casually through the exit door, but as he set foot outside he heard an authoritative voice say, 'Excuse me sir, would you mind coining back into the store?' Vernon turned. Two uniformed security officers stood there.

'What do you want? I've paid for my purchases.' But his voice was slightly high-pitched and sounded more of fear than in anger.

'Please sir, don't make this any more difficult than it is. Would you mind coming with us?' The following events seemed to take place quite rapidly, though he did notice that the guards had dropped the courtesy title of 'sir' and now addressed him as 'you'. They searched him and found the brandy. By this time, Vernon was in an agitated state. He gabbled out his words.

'Sorry I forgot that was in my pocket. I was going to pay for it at the checkout… I mean I'm quite willing to pay for it now…'

'Yes we suppose you are. So you forgot it was in your pocket, the only thing you forgot was the surveillance camera. Let us have your name and address. You'll remain here until the police arrive.'

The police gave Vernon the impression that the whole affair was like a well-rehearsed routine. They told him he would go before the magistrate within the next few days. Speed was essential when dealing with holidaymakers. The following Wednesday the sixth of July, Vernon appeared at the magistrates' court. He pleaded guilty because when he secreted the bottle of brandy in his jacket pocket he was recorded by the C.C.T.V. camera. He was fined, plus costs and damages to the supermarket.

He'd spent a worrying few days prior to his court appearance. Would his name and occupation be reported in his home town papers? He sought out the local reporter, a craggy old man with more miles on his clock than a vintage car, and asked him that question.

'I report all court proceedings to my paper, who then decide whether a case merits publication or not. However I don't think you need worry about my paper; because it is a local one, its readers are only interested in local people.' Vernon gave a loud sigh of relief. 'Although,' continued the reporter, 'all items of news are fed back to the press agencies so other newspapers, irrespective of their location, can print them.'

Vernon felt a wave of fear pass over him. He was on the point of asking the old hack how much he would take to supress the shoplifting offence but thought better of it. He reasoned that his good name and job were hanging on a thread, bribery would only make it worse.

'Then it looks as if I'll be out of a job tomorrow.'

The old reporter looked at Vernon in surprise.

'Surely a shoplifting offence is only a minor infringement of the law. They can't honestly sack you for that.'

'Oh yes they can. I'm a bank manager. I caused a young cashier to be dismissed for stealing ten pounds. It's fair to say that although I am respected in the bank I am not liked. There's quite a few who would enjoy pulling the trapdoor lever.'

'There is a chance, but it is only a longshot,' said the reporter, 'some sensational event might take place, like the assassination of John F. Kennedy or the bombing of Baghdad when the papers were crammed full of reports, interviews and photographs that left no room for trivial news items.' Vernon shook his head sadly, thanked the reporter and walked back to his hotel.

The following morning, Thursday the seventh of July 2005, he was up early and hurried down to the hotel lobby and bought five morning papers which he read avidly. He was pleased that there was no mention of 'Bank manager on shoplifting charge' or words to that effect. He ate his breakfast slowly, telling himself that the papers had gone to press before the syndicated news was available.

Vernon then made a decision and returned to his room and tried in vain to find a 'Do Not Disturb' sign so he turned on the radio because he felt the cleaners would not enter a room which was occupied. He then opened a jar of sleeping pills and recalled the advice from the pharmacist that the pills were very strong so it is imperative that he must not exceed the dose and above all never take the pills if you have been drinking alcohol.

The distraught bank manager gulped down several swigs of brandy and then swallowed a handful of pills at a time followed by further brandy chasers. He felt the pills were beginning to work and as the sleep of eternity crept over him he could still hear the radio announcer apologising for interrupting the programme, '…but there have been terrorist bomb explosions in London. One of these bombs exploded in an underground train with serious loss of life. Over to our reporter who is outside Liverpool Street Station…'

Peacefully

'Stand straight! You are charged with... oh never mind, you probably know why you are here.'

'But I don't...'

'Silence in court.'

'But this isn't a court!' He was aware that his voice was faltering, the person who seemed in charge appeared to be distant although his speech was strong and sounded quite near.

'When you address me, call me "your honour". I'm a judge.'

'But why do I have to wear this bulky overcoat and fur on my feet, your honour?'

'To keep you warm. Don't ask silly questions. In 1956 you were an office boy in Laccy's Shipping Co. and you gave cheek to the chief clerk Mr Robinson. That was on Friday the... er... oh never mind what date it was, it was in 1956, and over the following weekend Mr Robinson took his own life.'

'But I was not the cause of his suicide, the job was too much for him your hon...'

'I didn't say you were,' rapped the judge, 'but you obviously have strong feelings of guilt. Poor old Robbo, to end his life so tragically and no one suspected that impudent boy Henry...'

'I'm Harry.'

'Don't interrupt, we do not use familiarities here.'

Harry's mind was in a turmoil. The judge was shrouded in a kind of mist, but he did not appear to be wearing any wig or robes. The whole place looked nothing like a court and the so-called judge was seated at a plain ordinary table. Harry took courage and said, 'But I want to say something in my defence....'

'Be quiet, you'll have your chance to say all you want to, when the court has reached a guilty verdict.' By this time Harry could see the judge's features a little more clearly which, like his voice, were harsh and menacing.

'Remember Vera Duffy? You met her at a dance and took her home. It was obvious to you that she had too much to drink, but that did not stop you from taking advantage of her – in fact, in her inebriated state you knew you would have no difficulty in helping yourself.'

'She was willing to what happened.'

'Hold your tongue! I've not finished yet! It was not what you did that concerns this court but the way you reacted the next day in the local pub. With all your mates around, you gave a graphic account of what occurred. You boasted of how easy Vera was, and you added embellishments of your own, which were not entirely true. Her death was untimely and...'

'Death? Is she dead then? How, when?'

'Can't you guess, an overdose last week.'

'But that was years ago,' protested Harry.

'What was "last week"?' asked the judge.

'No, when I made love to her.'

'Made love to her eh? That wasn't the way you described it to your friends. You told them you shagged the arse off her and she couldn't get enough of it.'

'Well, I was young and single then, but why should something that happened over 35 years ago be responsible for her death?'

'You dubbed her a slut and it was the biggest single factor that caused Vera to eventually lose her self-respect.'

Harry started to feel vulnerable. The judge knew not only the events in detail but he was awakening thoughts he had long since pushed to the back of his mind.

'Do you remember Ron Taylor?'

'Oh yes, good old Ronnie, don't tell me he's topped himself?'

'No, nothing like that. You sneered, contradicted him and made a fool of him, especially in front of his colleagues.'

Harry's feelings of guilt gave way to resentment. 'Now hold on a minute, Ronnie was a good sport, anything I said was in fun.'

'Yes, good sport,' replied the judge, 'but extremely sensitive. You noticed when he was stooping down to get something out of his desk drawer, that the crown of his head was showing a little bald patch. "Looking forward to joining the monastery are we? With the circle of bare flesh on the top of your head you could pass off as a monk. You need to get into the Habit." When Ronnie rose to his feet you could tell you had touched a nerve, he was extremely embarrassed. Did that deter you? Oh no it didn't! Practically every morning from then on you would greet him with phrases like, "How's things at the monastery today?" On one occasion sitting around a table in the canteen there was Ronnie, two works colleagues, and yourself. Ronnie told a joke which did not receive much laughter and you noticed that this embarrassed him slightly. Like a vulture you dived in for the spoils, "Are you still speaking to the feller that told you that joke? If you tell corny jokes like that at home then I feel sorry for your long-suffering wife!"'

'I was only being friendly,' mumbled Harry. 'He didn't mind.'

The judge raised his voice, 'Mind? On the day we are discussing, Ronnie took it out on someone else, someone who was weaker than himself, his wife. An argument developed which ended up with Ronnie hitting his wife. The outcome of it all was the eventual break-up of the marriage.'

'But I'm not responsible for the break-up. I wasn't to know…'

'You should have curbed your sadistic desire to inflict pain,' interrupted the judge. 'When you sneer and use sarcasm, you elevate yourself by putting people down. As for compassion, you don't feel sorrow in any way, in fact you experience great delight in making others feel uncomfortable. Why is it in life you never admit you are in the wrong? When the situation arises that you are guilty of something, you go to great lengths explaining how you made the mistake but neve a word of apology.'

'I'm sure I do apologise sometimes.'

'No,' barked the judge, 'it is almost as though, to apologise for you is a sign of weakness.'

'I'm sorry,' said Harry, with head bowed.

'Enough of this. The sentence of the court is death. Ushers take him away.'

Two burly ushers grabbed Harry and hauled him from the court. Harry tried to struggle but found the bulky overcoat impeded his every movement and the coat was so long it got entangled in his feet. Try as he could, he could neither speak nor run free. He was bundled into a lift by the ushers and the judge, then whisked up to the top floor of what was a considerably high building. When the lift stopped, he was half carried along a passageway to a small room. The room, which was bare, had French windows that opened onto a balcony. Fear gripped him when he realised that he was to be thrown to his death from the balcony. Harry tried to struggle and shout, but his executioners were not only strong but seemed completely indifferent to his plight as they remorselessly went about their task. The executioners pushed him up on to the railing of the balcony and for a moment he was balanced on his stomach as they held his feet. He looked down and fear gave way to uncontrollable terror. He shouted out, pleading not to die as he grabbed the iron struts of the balcony. 'Over you go,' said one of the ushers, then added to the judge, 'He should be waking up now, shouldn't he?'

'Yes,' said the judge, 'any second now.' Then followed a scream of terror and a sickening thud.

'Good god!' exclaimed the usher, 'he didn't wake up. Is that unusual?'

'No,' answered the judge thoughtfully, 'but it happens sometimes, yes it does happen.'

'Will there be an investigation, I mean an inquest or something?' asked the usher.

'Of course not; all perfectly natural. I can visualise the death certificate now: "Cause of Death, Cardiac Arrest" and in his obituary or on his cemetery headstone will probably say something like "Henry Wilson, aged 63 years, passed away peacefully in his sleep…"'

Why Can't a Woman Converse Like a Man?

It's long been a belief of mine that women converse in a different language from men. No, I'm not referring to the almost enforced method of abbreviation used by many mothers to their children, like pinny for pinafore, jimjams for pyjamas, tummy for stomach, and so on but the way the fair sex convey their thoughts.

We attended a party the other week and since Pauline and me went by car, I was, like the party, boringly sober and should have been aware of everything that happened that night, so I was more than surprised when Pauline asked me later, 'What did you think of the fight?'

'What fight?'

'The head to head between Sheila and Jan.'

'Which one was Sheila? Was she the one with the big pair of…'

'Trust you to notice her figure.'

'I was going to say eyes, but those two didn't fight did they?'

There was a slight sound of enforced patience in Pauline's voice as though she was dealing with a naughty child.

'Well they didn't come to blows and hit one another, not in the way I wish to hit you right now. Surely you remember catty Sheila making a comment about Jan's dress?'

'Er yes I do remember that now, but it wasn't nasty.'

'You mean it didn't strike you as being a little unfriendly when Sheila told Jan that she always admired the style of her dress and so too did her grandmother.'

Pauline's words were like the slow motion replays in a televised football match, when you think the ref has given a wrong decision but the foul becomes obvious in the re-run.

'I don't suppose you recall Jan's reply?' I got that feeling of being a naughty child again as I shook my head.

'Well after the Sheila's put-down regarding Jan's dress, Jan very sweetly asked Sheila would she like to borrow it because she liked the style so much. She then added that of course Sheila would have to widen the waist a lot to make it fit!'

Sometimes it is not what is spoken by girls but the way it is said that conveys the meaning. During the party we met a couple, Freda and Jim, who were overjoyed at moving into their new house. As the time ticked away we decided to offer Freda and Jim a lift home, which they gratefully accepted. As we stopped outside the couple's home Freda asked us, 'Do you want to come in?'

I was just on the point of saying yes to the invitation, when Pauline cut in saying, 'Oh no thanks Freda, it is late and we both have to be up early tomorrow morning.'

After we drove away I asked Pauline why she had not accepted Freda's offer?

'Couldn't you tell she was only being polite. She had not been expecting visitors so she honestly wouldn't have welcomed showing virtual strangers around her house at two o'clock in the morning.'

'How could you tell?'

'By the way she asked.'

Perhaps in the use of language, intonation matters more to women than men. Females understand what is being said even when a question is obviously illogical. For example Pauline and me went to the theatre recently and during the interval we visited the bar which was crowded. However we were lucky enough to find a table and four empty chairs. Shortly after we had occupied two of the chairs, two women approached Pauline and pointing to the empty seats asked, 'Is anyone sitting there?' Pauline turned her head and looked at the empty chairs, looked back at the questioner and replied, 'Don't think so.'

Although Pauline had not met the ladies before, by the time the five-minute warning bell sounded, telling us that the show was about to continue, my wife and the two girls were chatting away like lifelong friends with little bits of gossip and humorous situations. If the two strangers had been men sitting at our table, my conversation would have been only politely friendly and much more reserved.

I remember Pauline answering the phone once and saying to the person at the other end of the line, 'no I'm Pauline. Oh hello Betty.' My better half then had a friendly chat lasting some twenty minutes with 'Betty'. After the call I asked Pauline out of curiosity who was on the phone.

'It was a wrong number.' Seeing my amused expression, she added, 'Well you can't be abrupt just because someone has dialled a wrong number.'

The difference in the way women use language is maybe why so many of them do not laugh at the same things as men. It is not fair to say the gentle sex has no sense of humour, it is just that their humour differs from men. Women are used to euphemisms and, when need be, irony. This is probably why females do not appreciate the quirky comedy in such shows as 'The Goons' and 'Monty Python' (I once knew a woman who described Monty Python as 'stupid stuff that clever people find funny). The reason why they do not laugh at the things men do is because they have a ballast of practicality and realism that prevents them enjoying a slightly twisted view of life.

I once heard a good joke told to me and couldn't get home quick enough to tell Pauline, about a man who found an old violin and a painting in his attic. He decided to take them round to an art dealer to see if they were worth anything.

The art dealer inspected the violin and painting and then said, 'Do you know what you have here, my man? You have a Stradivarius and a Rembrandt. Now don't get too excited because Stradivarius was a lousy painter and Rembrandt was useless at making violins.'

Pauline looked at me with a puzzled expression and said, 'Wouldn't the man have got a good price for the Stradivarius painting if only for the novelty value?'

Perhaps the fault is not in the joke but my bad delivery, although I know other men who can tell a joke well but seem to have the same problem.

Recently a friend of mine went round to see his aunt, and because she is a hairdresser he recounted a joke about a sailor who went into a barber's shop and asked the barber, 'How much for a crew cut?' The barber replied, 'A crew cut is six pounds.'

The sailor went to the door, opened it and shouted out, 'OK fellas, you can come in now.'

His aunt's expression did not change and after a short pause said, 'Go on.'

'That's it, Auntie, that's the joke.'

'Hmm, how is your mum these days? Is she still getting her migraine attacks?'

Then there is the girl who is so well mannered that when a man tells a joke, she will force a laugh so he will not be embarrassed (is that what you call faking it?).But even worse than that is what happened to my brother-in-law when he met a girl for the first time and told her a joke which she laughed at quite loudly saying, 'That was a good one, I must remember that.'

My brother-in-law felt very awkward – he hadn't finished the joke.

Although women have a good vocabulary they never seem to grasp sporting terminology. The other night I was watching a local Derby match on TV when I received a phone call. After I had finished the call I asked Pauline had anything happened while I was out of the room.

'Yes, the other side scored but it was cancelled.'

'What for?'

'He'd gone outside.'

'You mean he was offside.'

'Whatever.'

'Which player was offside?'

'The good looking one.'

'Which one was that?'

Pauline pointed him out, a player I disliked.

'You don't think he's good looking do you?'

'Oh yes he's nice.'

'Nice? If you think that gormless git is nice, then all I can say is you must have a queer taste in men.'

Pauline looked at me for second and then said, 'Yes I must have!'

The Audition

Joe licked his lips nervously as he waited for his interview. The theatrical agent's office was full of men hoping to gain a part in a remake of *Treasure Island.* What questions would they ask and who would get the plum part of Long John Silver? Joe had taken the trouble to read again Robert Louis Stevenson's classic story. Each time the door opened and a name was announced it was very much like being in the dentist's.

He looked round at the 'competition'; they were all out-of-work actors, although Joe preferred to use the phrase 'Resting between engagements'. At last Joe heard his name called. This was it. If only he could obtain a part in a big movie, fame and fortune would follow. As he entered the small office he was confronted by three men. One who seemed to be leader said, 'Now Joe, let us have your characterisation of Long John Silver.'

In a West Country accent he replied, 'Ah Jim lad, oy be glad to make your acquaintance, say hello to my parrot.'

The leader shouted out, 'Excellent, one more time.'

Joe obliged.

'Say, you have a fine voice, my boy. I don't think we need to go any further.' He looked at his two companions who nodded in agreement.

'Joe you've got the part of Long John Silver. You start next Tuesday. Your pay will be £3000.' Joe could hardly contain himself. '£3000 a week starting Tuesday? If you like I'll start on Monday.'

'Sorry, no can do. It will have to be Tuesday, because Monday you'll be in hospital having one of your legs amputated.'

Waiting

'Reliable Assurance Company,' said the recorded voice on the phone, 'to assist us to direct your call to the correct department, please use the numbers on your key phone pad as follows…'

Joe Baxter who was ringing to cancel his life policy listened carefully to his instructions.

'If you wish to renew your policy press number one, should you wish to make a claim press number two, change your direct debit press number three, increase your present cover press four…' and so the soulless operator's voice went on with all the personality of a speak-your-weight machine. Undaunted, Joe patiently waited and realised that there were only nine numbers on the phone pad, so the various options were nearing an end when the metallic voice reached number eight, then the next one would be the last and surely the one for people wanting to cancel their policy, but NO, number nine was for those who wished to donate their organs for the benefit of medical science.

Joe, a man of quiet resolve reviewed the situations open to him and reasoned that since he was going to cancel his policy, then it followed that the direct debit would have to be changed as well, so he would tap in the number three.

A few clicks emanated from the earpiece then the impersonal voice of the same operator said, 'Please tap in your policy number on the phone pad so we can have your file details to hand when you are connected.' Joe obliged and was told, 'We are sorry, all our representatives are busy talking to customers at present but as soon as one is free we shall put you through. Your call is important to us.' There then followed some recorded music with 'inter-round summaries' from the 'speaking clock' voice saying, 'All our representatives are still busy with customers, we shall connect you as soon as one is free. Your call is important to us.'

This last phrase gave Joe some hope, despite the fact he was resigned to a long wait. Slowly the seconds ticked by followed by the minutes and then the hours became days, but Joe grimly hung on until the good Lord up above relieved Joe of his suffering. Then a voice came on the telephone, not a recorded voice but a real live human voice, 'Hello Mr Joseph Baxter, sorry you have had to wait so long, how can I help you?'

'No, I'm not Joseph Baxter, I'm his son. My dad died about a week ago.'

'Oh, I am sorry to hear that, please accept my sincere condolences, but you are onto the wrong department, you need "Claims", so I suggest you replace your receiver and dial again and the operator will give you some options. Simply press the number two and wait.'

A Desirable Residence

'It would be ideal for a student such as you. I know it's old and rundown but the rent is cheap and it is fairly isolated so you won't be disturbed when you study.' I recalled these words by Mr. Johnson, the estate agent as I approached an old dilapidated house which was set apart from any other building in a country lane. The rent was ridiculously low and I remember asking Mr. Johnson, 'What's the catch?'

To which he tactfully changed the subject and I began to wonder if there was a more sinister reason why the house had been left unoccupied for so long. 'Is the house haunted?' I asked.

He smiled at me disarmingly and then said, 'Well there are rumours that previous events are re-enacted from time to time but that shouldn't bother a young fit student like you.' When I enquired what these events were he refused to be drawn. Despite my misgivings about the place the affordable rent prompted me to close the deal.

The stone driveway leading up to the front of the house was over-run with weeds and they seemed to be pushing their heads up between the paving stones as though they needed fresh air. The door was old and thirsting for a couple of coats of paints. When I opened it, it groaned and creaked in protest, and I remember thinking that the people who make those horror films; would pay good money for an atmospheric door like this. Inside the house the rooms were cold with the smell of decaying wood. There was little or no furniture to be seen and this did not make the property in anyway homely. Upstairs the bedrooms were even colder than downstairs. The floorboards voiced their objection to being walked on and the walls and ceilings were yellowed by years of tobacco smoke. Windows were dirty and cracked, and it was then that I started to wonder if renting the house had been a wise move.

I managed to light a fire and brewed some tea with an old-fashioned kettle and teapot I found in the kitchen. The tea with some sandwiches and the warmth of the fire made life a little more bearable. Using my overcoat together with a blanket from my backpack I was able to make an adequate cover on a rusty bed, so I settled down to spend a primitive night in the old house. I had tried before this to read some of my text books, but I was tired and lacked enthusiasm to study.

I rested my head on the backpack which served as a substitute pillow. I listened to the wind whistling tunelessly through the cracks and holes in the walls. When the wind subsided, I could hear the creak of the carpet-less stairs as though someone big and heavy was walking slowly up them. This was followed by a low moan, was that the wind or an anguished cry of a troubled soul? Ghostly voices seemed to be talking to one another. Suddenly there came a swish of what sounded like a whip or belt and the cries of pain from an unknown man as he received his punishment, then all was quiet.

I managed to doze off, but was awakened by what sounded like a person fighting for breath. Shrieks of hysterical laughter echoed round the room. Against this mixture of sounds I began to realise that the house must have been a lunatic asylum many years ago when they cruelly punished the mentally disturbed inmates to cure them. I resolved to vacate the premised the following day. Mercifully, the noises of the night ceased and allowed me to sleep.

Next morning, the sun streamed through the windows lighting up the dingy bedroom and painting the ugliness of the property with beauty. I decided to inspect the premises and found the passing of years had been gentle on the old house, because in the light of day it had a certain charm. The hall or reception room had a very tall ceiling and the walls showed square patches where pictures once hung. Other rooms were large and everywhere there was a prevailing odour of mustiness... In the rear of the house was another staircase that ran up to the attic and was probably the servants' quarters.

I tried to visualise how the place looked in the 19th century, especially when the owners were entertaining. This of course was before it was used as a place for mentally ill people. I could imagine liveried footmen driving carriage and horses up the driveway and stopping at the front door. Guests would alight from the leather-upholstered seats, a picture of elegance. Ladies would be resplendent in beautiful gowns and the gentlemen would be dressed in top hat and tails; all would be a vision of Victorian opulence, but my reverie ended abruptly when I heard a knocking at the front door.

I opened the door and was pleased to see Mr Johnson. Was it my imagination but did he seem a little apprehensive?

'Well, what sort of a night did you have, young man?'

'Oh, not too bad. Tell me Mr Johnson, the fact that no one had offered to buy or rent this place, is that because of what it was used for?'

'Yes, I must confess that had a great bearing on it.'

'Then I was right, Mr Johnson. I heard during the night sounds of people being beaten, shrieks of hysterical laughter and other noises of inmates fighting for breath. Was this place a lunatic asylum?'

Mr Johnson raised his eyebrows and his face relaxed into a smile.

'No, young man, it was a Victorian brothel.'

www.ingramcontent.com/pod-product-compliance
Ingram Content Group UK Ltd.
Pitfield, Milton Keynes, MK11 3LW, UK
UKHW042002190726
13854UKWH00005B/2118